© Editorial Playor

Adapted and published in the
United States in 1985 by
Silver Burdett Company,
Morristown, New Jersey

1985 Printing

ISBN 0-382-09096-9   (Lib. Bdg)
ISBN 0-382-09102-7

Library of Congress
Catalog Card Number 85-40434

Depósito legal: M. 33.190-1985
Edime, S. A. - Móstoles (Madrid)
Printed in Spain

Silver Burdett Company

CLASSICS FOR KIDS

A TALE FROM THE ARABIAN NIGHTS

Adapted for young readers by Vincent Buranelli

illustrated by Hieronimus Fromm

A beautiful princess named Scheherazade married a king who had each of his wives executed on the day after the wedding. To prevent this from happening to her, Scheherazade told the king a different story every night.

He was so fascinated by her stories that he allowed her to go on for a thousand and one nights. And he allowed her to live after that. So, Scheherazade saved her head with such brilliant stories as "Sinbad the Sailor" and "Aladdin and His Wonderful Lamp."

One of her best stories was "The Tale of the Talking Bird, the Singing Tree and the Water that was Made of Gold." It told of a sultana, the wife of a sultan, who had three wicked sisters.

When three children were born to the sultan and the sultana, the wicked sisters put them into a basket, and threw the basket into the river.

But the three babies were lucky. Near the long, deep river there lived a kind gardener named Koruschan. He went to the river one night to fetch some water for his garden's flowers. He found the floating basket. And in it, he saw three beautiful children, two boys and a girl.

Koruschan carried the babies to his house. He took care of them until they were grown. He named the boys Baman and Parvis, and he called the girl Parizade.

Parizade was very kind, and one day she invited a mysterious old man to her house. She gave him something to eat and the old man said he liked the house and the garden very much.

But then he told the children that three things were missing in their house that would make their happiness complete: the talking bird, the singing tree, and the water that was made of gold. He told them that they would find these three things near the place where an ancient man with a white beard was sitting.

Baman and Parvis decided to look for the three wonders. Parizade would stay at home. The old man gave her a flower. He told her that if Baman and Parvis were in danger, the flower would begin to bleed.

Baman and Parvis came to the place where the ancient man with the white beard was sitting. The two brothers asked him where the three wonders were to be found.

The ancient man with the white beard said to them: "Take this ball and throw it. Follow it until it stops rolling and, where it stops, you will see many black rocks. The rocks will call to you and tell you to return to your house. But don't be afraid of them and don't look back, because if you do, you two will be turned into black rocks. Keep walking and you will find the talking bird. Ask him, and he will tell you where to find the singing tree and the water that is made of gold."

Meanwhile, Parizade had noticed that the flower which the mysterious old man had given to her had begun to bleed. That meant that her brothers were in danger, so Parizade got on her horse and rode to the place where the ancient man with the white beard was sitting. He told her that Baman and Parvis had been turned into black rocks because they had looked back when the rocks had called to them.

The ancient man with the white beard also told her that she could save them from the enchantment only if she found the talking bird, the singing tree, and the water that was made of gold. Brave, beautiful Parizade did what he told her. She found the three marvels.

Baman and Parvis had been turned into black rocks just as the ancient man with the white beard had said. There they stood among the other black rocks, sadly thinking that Parizade would never be able to rescue them. But they did not know that Parizade had already found the talking bird.

This strange creature had told her to take one of the singing tree's branches and plant it in her garden. The bird also told her to take a silver cup filled to the brim with the water that was made of gold. If she poured it over her brothers, they would become boys again.

So, Parizade poured the water that was made of gold on her brothers. When she did this, the black rocks magically disappeared and Baman and Parvis felt free and full of life again. The two brothers hugged their sister and the three started eagerly on their way home. They wanted to enjoy the three wonders Parizade had found.

They poured a few drops of water into their garden's fountain and suddenly, all its water was turned into gold. Its flow never stopped. They planted the branch and, in the garden, there grew a beautiful tree which never stopped singing many lovely songs. The talking bird would tell the two brothers and the sister the most wonderful stories in the world. That's why the house in which the two princes and the princess lived with Koruschan became the most fascinating house in the world.

One day the sultan happened to walk in front of the house. The poor sultan had never forgotten the loss of his children. Since the day that they had disappeared, he had been very sad. Yet, he felt cheered by the lovely music and happy songs that came from the strangely beautiful tree in Koruschan's garden. The sultan wanted to learn more about the tree, and about the beautiful girl he had seen standing by the window.

When the sultan walked into the house, Baman, Parvis, and Parizade were in the garden. The sultan's surprise when he saw the talking bird was indescribable. And can you imagine how happy he became when that same talking bird told him that the two brothers and the sister were his children!

The bird told the sultan all about the sultana's wicked sisters who had thrown the three babies into the river. He also told him all about Koruschan who had saved them and loved them.

The sultan and the sultana became happy again. They gave Koruschan many magnificent gifts for the loving way he had treated their children. They told him he could live with them in the palace. The wicked sisters were punished for what they had done. All the people celebrated by listening to the singing tree's lovely songs. Everyone loved the talking bird's stories. And, whenever anybody got sick, they would drink the water that was made of gold and become well again.